A HORROR THRILLER

A PEACEFUL TOWN

ALEXANDER SEMENYUK

This is a work of fiction. Names, characters, places, and incidents are products of the author's imagination or are used fictitiously and are not to be construed as real. Any resemblance to actual events, locations, organizations, or persons, living or dead, is entirely coincidental.

World Castle Publishing, LLC
Pensacola, Florida
Copyright © 2023 Alexander Semenyuk
Paperback ISBN: 9798891260245
eBook ISBN: 9798891260252
First Edition World Castle Publishing, LLC, August 14, 2023
http://www.worldcastlepublishing.com

Licensing Notes

Cover: Karen Fuller

Dedicated to all of the children in Ukraine who are suffering.

CHAPTER 1
HE COMES AT NIGHT

Cute little Soby, a tiny dog, trotted happily out into his cozy backyard, as he did every evening, to do his business with a smile on his face.

But tonight, he was terrified as he noticed two red eyes staring at him from the hedge. Before he could yelp or turn and run, a deformed coyote leaped out as quick as lightning and snatched him with razor-sharp teeth. There was just a little whimper. Ever so faint....

Dory, the old lady who owned him, called and called all night long, but of course, there wasn't a reply.

***

My name is Paul Thompkins. I am a retired Marine, now a hunter. Right now, I am busy with another task. In the early morning, I was walking around the town, putting up flyers about my dog, who was missing. Soma was a large and powerful wolf dog—who had been a longtime companion. I was close to tears as I went about my task.

When I finished posting flyers on each street and getting some sympathetic remarks from some passersby, I entered the coffee shop. It was a nice, welcoming place with a retro-style dark red interior. I got regular black coffee with a drop of whole milk and a slice of toast. As I sat by a funny retro coffee poster: "Coffee helps me pretend you're interesting," I listened to the sheriff make an announcement on the local radio station.

"This is the fifth dog that's gone missing from its yard at night. All five were small breeds, and there was blood found in each yard. We strongly suspect there is a wolf in the area."

Chills ran down my spine. Had Soma gone insane and started killing little dogs?!

No…not my good boy, no chance. I finished the coffee faster than usual and hastened home. I knew what had to be done.

My old hunting gear still looked great. With a heavy heart, I dressed in camouflage, made sure my rifle was all ready for its work, and set out into the forest that bordered the town. Whatever had taken those dogs would love the bloody steak I carried with me.

I went far into the leafy depths. The

sun was rather bright, which was a good sign. I tied the large raw steak to a low tree branch and situated myself uphill, ready to fire.

Waiting was my forte. I loved to wait. In fact, I had probably done too much waiting in my life, but today my patience would come in handy.

Two hours passed before I heard movement in the bushes. I was ready.

But I was taken by surprise. Crazy pain shot through my body as something grabbed my shoulder from behind. I fell down the hill and rolled, eventually getting stuck between two short trees. The rifle slid away, and my left arm went numb. Right above me stood the biggest coyote I'd ever seen. His eyes were bloodshot, and saliva dripped profusely from his disgusting mouth. He was about to kill me.

As he moved in, a large wolf-dog

grabbed his neck from the side and pushed him down. The coyote tried to get away, but it was too late. The wolf-dog had a strong grip on his neck with his jaws. I heard a cracking sound.

Soma was always abnormally strong. The coyote's body convulsed on the ground and then lay motionless.

Soma slowly came up to me and licked my face.

"The steak did work, after all! It was you who came for it, though the coyote came for me. Good job, Soma... good boy."

Needless to say, Soma became the town's hero, and I became the joke. That's okay with me, really. I got my dog back, and the town was peaceful again.

CHAPTER 2
RATTY BUSINESS

The quiet town of Gravil was almost a paradise. It had gorgeous blue mountains on one side, a thick green forest on the other, and a beautiful lake just a short hike away.

Yet, in this town of eight thousand residents, recent developments had upset the delicate balance of things. First, a coyote terrorized the community. It was finally caught by a local hunter, Paul, and his brave dog, Soma. Then, just weeks later, the police department announced that they had found two missing teens, both dead, and each missing a left ear. Not wanting to set off a panic, they had kept it quiet after the first victim but had to tell the community after the second body was found. Now there was the possibility that a serial killer had come to town.

You think that's it?

Unfortunately, yet another tragedy struck. A nearby factory specializing in radioactive materials and toxic chemicals went up in flames, taking the lives of the workers and leaving only one survivor, a man named Kevin.

The country's government sent many specialists to examine the site, contain any leaks, and ensure that the water supply was not contaminated. They did well, which surprised the citizens since they were skeptical about the way government workers had handled similar situations in the region in the past.

However…a tiny bit of trouble emerged from the factory. Then the tiny thing became a big thing.

A huge radioactive rat was spotted leaving the house of a local milkman, and when police arrived, they found the man dead inside.

Detective Pirel was the town's top detective. He was disturbed to find that there were other, normal rats lying dead near the house.

In the coming days, reports of dead rats were piling up. The townspeople once again were frightened and highly strung. Pirel could feel the anxiety and tension in the air.

The only well-known animal tracker in town was none other than Paul, with his wolf-dog Soma.

Pirel felt bad asking for assistance, but Paul was over the moon at his request.

And so, the hunt began.

It was a beautiful morning. The gorgeous orange sun was just peeking from behind the mountains when Pirel heard a knock on his door and jumped out of bed, startled. He glanced at the clock.

"Six? Oh no…."

Was there another victim, and his phone was not working? He quickly picked up his phone and saw that the screen had no messages. Huh. The knock came again.

"Coming, coming."

He quickly threw on a black jacket and swiftly pulled on his black pants. To his surprise, when he opened the door, he discovered Paul standing there with two large coffees and Soma behind him.

Paul nodded at the detective. "I

have some bread, too. You want to catch this rat, then we gotta go early. I have an idea where it might be going each night."

Pirel nodded, and they sat at the table by the window. The dog dropped himself on the floor with a thud.

Indicating Soma, Pirel said, "Should he really be going with us?"

Paul grinned. "Of course, my dear Mr. Pirel, This dog will lead us straight to the monster."

"So where is this place we are going to?"

After taking a large swallow of coffee, Paul answered, "Not far from the old factory is the sewer's exit pipe. There is also farmland nearby, with plenty to eat for a rat. I believe it goes back there."

"Makes sense." Pirel chewed some bread.

"How about the serial killer case?"

Pirel blinked hard and rubbed his

forehead. "Uh, I think we went too early with that title, as the two victims might have known each other. This could have been a grudge or a revenge sort of thing. Maybe they bullied someone. So, there may be no serial killer after all."

"Are the rumors true? They had their left ears cut off?" Paul asked.

"Yes, but don't tell anyone about what I speak of between us, please."

"Of course."

Paul was surprised when Pirel continued, "The ears are not the weirdest thing about the case. Both victims died of heart attacks, and there were no other injuries on the bodies besides the left ear missing."

"What does that mean? Both were truly terrified? Scared to death? The ears were cut off while they were still alive?"

Pirel heaved a sigh. "Possibly all of the above. Uh, I got a lot on my plate right now. The town's troubles went from zero to sixty in an instant, it seems."

"Well, shall we go?"

Pirel nodded, and they went to Paul's truck. The drive was pleasant. Soma stuck his head out of the window, enjoying the fresh air. They had to park about a ten-minute walk from the pipe exit.

When they reached the location, Paul instantly had a satisfied look on his face. He pointed out animal droppings near the pipe.

"Rat, but larger than usual."

They heard Soma barking a short way to the left. As they hurried over, they saw several dead rats with torn throats.

"This rat doesn't like to share."

Pirel suddenly looked more grim than before. "Paul, isn't there a small trailer community nearby?"

"Oh my God, yes, there is. Do you

think they are ok?"

"We will find out now. Let's get back in the car."

It was a short drive to the small trailer park. When they stopped the truck, both of them noticed instantly that it was unusually quiet. There were five trailer homes in total, but no one outside.

"Help me!"

The cry came from some shrubbery encircling the trailers. They ran as quickly as they could and found a boy there with his right leg completely mutilated. He was shaking and sweating from pain.

"It…it ran when it heard you!" He pointed behind him.

Pirel turned to Paul.

"Take the boy to the hospital, but first drop me off near the pipe. We can beat the rat to its lair, and I can hide and wait for it."

Paul was at the wheel now, and

Soma was trying his best to comfort the injured boy lying in the back seat. The moment they reached the area near the pipe, Pirel jumped out, waved to them and ran.

Pirel reached the pipe and hid in the thick underbrush, holding his gun. He began slowing down his breathing and calming his heart rate.

"Calm down, calm down," he whispered to himself.

To Pirel's frustration, even after an hour, there was no sign of the rat, but on the bright side, he was totally calm.

Several more hours passed. He received some messages from Paul and briefly replied, telling Paul to stay at the hospital with the boy. He had to be focused.

As his eyes began to droop, he finally heard a rustling coming from the forest. The rat was there, moving rather slowly. It was the size of a dog now, a truly ugly and disturbing creature with blood on its mouth. Its body was swaying slightly from side to side as it ambled toward the pipe. Had it eaten too much?

Pirel took aim. A single shot, right between the eyes. Blood splashed on the grass, and the rat's body flew back a bit. Pirel approached it with care and attention, ready to fire again. He rarely missed. As a former national shooting champion, for Pirel, rarely meant never. Yet he always took a professional approach, and this time was no exception. He stood above the rat, examining it. The freaky thing was indeed dead. He sighed with relief and put away the gun, looking up at the sky.

Lesson here?

Gluttony really will kill you.

CHAPTER 3
CHERNOBYL MAN

Ah, the good town of Gravil. Peaceful blue mountains, fresh air, fields that seem endless, and a gorgeous, calm lake to soothe the soul.

How sad it is that this beautiful little town hides a man with a heart of black ice. A killer who has no respect for other human beings. Someone who does not care about the pain and the tears of his victims' relatives. A man who enjoys tormenting others.

He has perfectly blended into the town.

Even more sad is the fact that the suspicions of the town have fallen on the wrong person in recent times: The only man who survived the catastrophe at the factory.

Kevin was always a hard-working man. His kind heart endured many hardships, and he always remained faithful to his wife and a good father to his daughter. However, since the factory incident, things began to change for Kevin.

At first, a week after the disaster, Kevin woke up at four a.m. He found himself fully awake. He tried to go back to sleep, yet there was a tremendous pain behind his eyes as he tried to close them. He stood up and watched his family sleep, confused. He had always been a sound sleeper.

Kevin spent that whole morning sitting by the window, waiting. He expected to be exhausted, but in fact, it was the opposite. Even his family was surprised as he cooked the meals, helped clean the house, took the dog out one extra time and played soccer with his daughter.

Night came, and Kevin thought he'd sleep like a baby, yet this time he woke up even earlier.

Disturbed, he saw the clock indicate that it was two a.m. When he tried to sleep, the result was the same...terrifying pain behind his eyes. He walked around the house, pacing nervously.

What was going on? Was he losing his mind? Or had the radioactive spill changed him?

It had changed him, all right. The following night Kevin was unable to sleep at all. Little did he know that he would never sleep again in his life.

After several nights Kevin's anxiety started to ease, and he made the decision to look at things positively. He prepared breakfast for the family, took the dog out earlier, cleaned the kitchen quietly in the night and started gardening.

What if this strange change were, in fact, a blessing, not a curse? Kevin realized that he could start making a bigger difference in the community, and so he volunteered to be the town's clean-up guy without telling anyone. However, this was not a brilliant idea.

As young teens continued to go missing, people in town started noticing a man creeping around at night. Kevin was cleaning up all kinds of trash, washing windows, and making sure outdoor public gardens and trails were in order. Anything he could do at night, he did. And he seemed to have endless energy.

Kevin was happy about his efforts to help the town. He had no idea that his movements were suspect until the police came knocking on his door. Investigator Pirel and two officers asked to enter the house and speak to him. Kevin had no problem with this.

Kevin was devastated when he learned that his nighttime work made him a prime suspect. For several nights in a row, Kevin went to sit by the lake. On the second night, two major events unfolded. Sadly, he did not realize how important one of them was until much later in our story.

As Kevin sat by the lake, looking at the moon's reflection, someone spoke right behind him. He was so startled he almost fell into the water. He turned frantically and looked. There, by an oak tree, stood a man in all black, with wavy long hair of the same dark color as his jacket.

"Hello, Kevin, it's a nice night out," the man said.

"Oh…wait, you're that French painter!"

The man smiled. "Correct, that's me, good old Pierre." Pierre wore a strange smile as he said "old," for he actually looked very young.

"Why are you here at night, Pierre?"

"I like the night. That's when I'm at my best. I paint at night too."

"You don't sleep?" Kevin asked, surprised.

"Oh, I sleep all right. I'm not…like you."

"How do you know how I am? Have the rumors about me spread so quickly?"

Pierre smiled, but his eyes were cold. "Oh no, I just know, don't you worry. I know you're not the killer."

"Why do you say that?" Kevin asked, incredulously. Kevin's heart began to race. Was Pierre himself the killer?

The other man chuckled. "No, no. I'm not the killer, either. I know who is, however."

Kevin's mouth dropped open. "What, how, who? Why aren't you going to the police?"

A whisper of a smile lifted Pierre's lips. "The matters of humans...sorry, I mean in matters such as these, these affairs, they must play out on their own. I have no right to interfere." He shrugged. "It was nice seeing you here, Kevin."

Kevin shook his head angrily and looked away for a moment. He turned back to give Pierre a mouthful about moral responsibilities, but the man had vanished. Kevin got up and quickly walked along the shore, trying to see in the dark. No sign of Pierre. However, he noticed someone else heading up a far hill. The slim, tall man wore an all-white outfit, which was the reason he caught Kevin's eye. Just as he was about to run after him, Kevin noticed something else.

Flames were coming from something a ways off to his right. The Jacksons' farmhouse was on fire! Was the family inside?

Kevin broke into a run and reached the front door. He pounded on it, yelling to see if anyone was at home. He kicked at the door until it broke open and ran inside.

From one of the upstairs rooms came a faint scream. Kevin pulled his shirt up over his nose and mouth and ran through the acrid smoke up the stairs. He slammed his body into that door, too, and rushed inside the room to find the Jacksons' ten-year-old son. The kid looked terrified.

"Are your parents home?"

"Their car broke down. They had to stay at Grandma's overnight."

Kevin slung the boy over his shoulder and carried him out. As they got safely away from the house, the roof collapsed, and the flames roared higher. Kevin had no clue how he'd call for help, yet he heard sirens. Someone else had called. Holding the boy, he turned away so the kid could not see his home in ruins and noticed Pierre watching from a nearby rise in the ground. Pierre gave Kevin a smile and a thumbs-up. Confused yet grateful, Kevin answered the same way.

The next day the whole town was aware that Kevin had saved the boy. Suspicions no longer followed him, and people were buying him coffee and pastries at the town's famous Tojo Brew cafe.

As Kevin sat at the table with family and new friends, he looked out the café window. He saw a tall, slim, handsome man in an all-white suit walk out of an alleyway. The man stopped for a moment and looked back at Kevin with an expression of disapproval on his face. Because of the fire, Kevin had forgotten about seeing someone else near the lake…in an all-white outfit….

The town came up with a new nickname for Kevin. Chernobyl Man.

The next day police found another murder victim, a young girl, tied to a tree not far from where Kevin had spoken with Pierre. Her left ear had been cut off.

That very same day, the slim man in white slowly strolled the cobblestone streets. A smile played upon his face as he held a bag of fresh celery in his left hand.

Life in Gravil was good for him.

CHAPTER 4
BIRD OF DEATH

The Gravil mountains were known by many as "treacherous beauties." Over the years, many of those who ventured far into them never came back.

I, however, seemed to have found a sweet spot where I was safe and yet still had a great view of the entire town and valley. Or so I thought....

It was a typical day for me. After completing my very important routine, I needed to dump something at the foot of the mountain, and I conveniently brought my lunch basket with me.

The sun sat high. Warm rays showered my skin as I made my way up a rocky path, trying not to get my white suit dirty. I had several white suits, so it wouldn't be a tragedy, yet I hated to wear anything dirty. Even if it was just a smudge, it drove me crazy. I had to be neat. If my socks ever had a thread come out, I threw them away. I never tried to wash out stains either; I just got rid of the clothes since they weren't perfect anymore.

I was indeed successful in getting to my spot without getting any dirt on myself. I spread out a black blanket near a large rock and sat down. The view from here was magnificent. The whole town, the lake, the river, and the gorgeous fields were all laid out right in front of me. Perfect nature pieces and amazing art.

I was, of course, sort of an artist myself. I had a very different style, but I was an artist nevertheless. An artist of life and death, and my new collection was beautiful.

I opened up my lunch basket. It held a perfectly pure, clean meal. Celery sticks, almonds, broccoli, spinach, coconut water and a handful of sunflower seeds. All organic, of course. Mmmm…I took a big bite out of the celery stick.

Refreshing!

My enjoyment was sadly cut short when I heard a strange sound behind me. It was a rustling noise, indicating movement.

I turned and observed the large pile of rocks sitting right above a line of thick shrubs. The rocks were moving, like someone was digging behind them for some reason. I slowly put away my food, neatly closed the box again and stood up.

"Hey! What are you doing here? It's not a good idea to ruin my lunch!"

The rock movement stopped. I scared them, ha! But that was not it.

A few seconds passed, and then the gigantic head of a strange black bird emerged. It had a long sharp beak and large yellow eyes, and as it fully stood up, it towered over the rocks and over me. I stood still, but my heart was pounding.

Suddenly the bird let out a scream and charged at me. I jumped to the side and rolled behind a large boulder. The bird swooped down and grabbed the blanket and basket. I briefly glimpsed my suit's sleeves.

Damned bird! My clothes were getting dirty! Dirty!

Before I knew it, the bastard was coming back around, screaming in its disgusting voice. Okay….

I began to frantically run down the trail. I could hear it right behind me.

As I reached flat land, a sharp pain shot through my body as I felt claws rip at my right shoulder. Blood sprayed down the side of my perfect white suit.

In anger and desperation, I dashed into the forest and dived into the underbrush.

Damn it…that bird ruined my lunch, my suit and my skin!

The creature flew up in a circle, then landed and began walking around, poking its beak into the bushes. My heart raced as adrenaline coursed through my body, not out of fear but because of what this bastard had done to me, especially my suit. I reached for my inner pocket.

"I got a surprise for you, bastard. You're gonna love it."

But then, before I could take any

action, the bird's head swiveled away from me.

A large black bear was ambling through the forest, looking like he'd just eaten.

Well, his lunchtime was about to be ruined also. As the bird charged at him, I didn't stick around for details and ran towards the town.

I was hurrying home to my little corner when I heard a voice.

"Mr. Usseti, what happened to you?"

Irritated, I turned. It was the damned baker, an ugly, fat man. I wanted to yell at him, but I was a gentleman.

"Everything is fine, just a bad lunch experience. I just...had a fall. Good day to you, kind sir." I waved him away.

Needless to say, I needed a new lunch spot.

CHAPTER 5
SNAKE ISLAND

Usseti sat at a small table outside of a health food shop. His juicer was broken and while the new one was on the way he had to suffer walking to this shop for his juice. His shoulder still hurt from the ordeal with the freaky bird, and he still had no idea where his new lunch spot would be. Though he kept a placid, benevolent look on his face, he looked around at others with disdain.

He especially hated the coffee

drinkers. They were lousy people, addicts. He particularly disliked a man named Tomasso. This chubby, short guy dared to have an Italian last name as he did, yet the man was a slob. Tomasso loved coffee, never trained, rarely shaved, and wore shabby clothes.

How can someone live like that? Just kill yourself! thought Usseti as he watched Tomasso cross the street. Little did he know that the short man was about to do so — in a way.

Tomasso had stolen from the mob in the big city the week before and naively thought he would get away with it. But as he turned toward his apartment in an alley, suddenly, several tall men in black suits appeared, blocking his way.

He charged at the men, not realizing that he looked like a sloth charging at a lion.

The men grabbed him, and before

he could even yell, they taped his mouth shut and tied his hands. Then they stuffed him into a large black van and began the long drive back to the big city.

***

The mob boss was in a particularly foul mood, though not because of Tomasso. He had just found out that his teenage daughter had a boyfriend. He sat brooding, smoking one of his endless cigars, with a glass of whiskey at his elbow. When the call came that Tomasso was on his way, he thought of a particularly gruesome way to punish him.

The mob boss requested his helicopter to be ready upon Tomasso's arrival. He was going to give that fool a very special treat.

The henchmen dragged Tomosso, his eyes wide with fear, toward the helicopter. They shoved him into the machine, which took off. Tomasso whimpered through his gag.

Cigar clamped between his teeth, the mob boss grinned evilly. "Well, well. My petty little thief. Take off that tape."

One of the men ripped the rape from Tomasso's mouth, and he let out a yell. "Please, sir, I didn't...," The boss silenced him with a hard smack across the face.

"Don't speak out of order. You thought you were smarter than us? Heh. Gravil? You think that was smart? I even own a business there. You really are an idiot. A greedy idiot." He narrowed his eyes, smoke rising from his stogie.

"Usually, I'd dispose of you quickly, but I'm taking you to a special place. There is an island where for every square meter on average, there are two snakes. Imagine that? It's almost unbelievable.

"I've taken a guy there before. He lay there, not moving, starving to death. Finally, he tried his luck with that depleted body, and the snakes got him. He's still there, all right. You'll see his corpse."

Tomasso was shaking and sweating in terror. The helicopter had reached the sea. In the distance, he could see a small island.

"There it is!" the mob boss cried.

No matter how much Tomasso pleaded, asked, and sobbed, he was still lowered onto the island.

***

Did the crime really merit the punishment? Usseti surely would think so. As all of this conspired many miles away, the sun was starting to set on the town of Gravil. Usseti prepared to attend a gallery opening later that night. The painter, Pierre's work would be exhibited. Usseti really did appreciate other artists, and he did not want to miss it.

However…the urge was powerful….

He stood at the corner of the street, watching the residents of the peaceful town going about their business. Who could be part of his art?

He shook his head.

I really want to see Pierre's gallery, he thought. But the urge…it was so strong! He began to laugh quietly, leaning his head against a brick wall.

A peaceful town…A lovely peaceful town….

It was so perfect for him. Here he could enjoy his art, unbothered and lead a peaceful life.

CHAPTER 6
THE BLOODY PAINTER

Pierre stood by the window. It was almost time for his exhibit. He enjoyed the season when the sun set earlier, as that meant he could be out earlier as well.

As he stood there, he noticed an old couple crossing the street to reach their nice little white house with a wide front porch. Pierre slowly looked into the mirror on the wall to his right.

So young, yet so old.

The ever-youthful face looked back

at him, frozen forever at 17 years old.

Outside, it began to rain, and Pierre's mind traveled far, far away, into the land of distant memories. It had happened so long ago, yet it was still so clear in his mind.

He was in the cottage in a small, old French village. His parents, simple farmers, sat at the dinner table with him. There were candles lit, and he remembered how happy he was because, on that particular night, his father had brought tomatoes. They were slicing them and eating them on bread.

Pierre still remembered how they'd tasted—a memory that stuck with him for eternity. His final meal as a human.

That night a band of thieves had come into the village, and sadly for Pierre, they targeted his home first. His parents had run out when they heard strange noises near the henhouse. They were instantly attacked, and Pierre rushed outside to help, but he was a thin and timid-looking young man. One of the robbers stabbed him in the stomach, and he collapsed to his knees. He watched as his parents were stabbed to death and the house set on fire. Then the robbers turned to finish him off. But with a last ounce of strength, Pierre ran into the tall grassy fields. Then he fell. He could hear the thieves coming for him, but he could no longer move. He lay on his back, awaiting death.

Death did come, but not in the way he thought it would. He heard the robbers screaming as they approached. And then silence.

Slowly a tall, pale man appeared right above him. He calmly knelt next to Pierre and propped up his head. "You are the young man who saved my great-great-granddaughter from drowning. I don't know if this is right or wrong, but I can't let you die like this."

Pierre briefly remembered pulling a little girl out of a river. Then the last thing he remembered as a human was a warm liquid pouring down his throat.

Pierre came back to the present moment. There were tears in his eyes. He slowly wiped them and watched himself in the mirror. "Sometimes we think what we are doing is noble, but to someone else, it's a terror," he whispered, wryly.

Since that day, Pierre had endured a painful life. His only food was blood. Though on principle, he refused to kill humans, except on a few occasions, he'd had to do it. He hunted and drank the blood of all kinds of animals. It wasn't ideal, but it aligned with his morals.

In the recent few decades, he had found something that helped him live a better life.

It was art. Painting.

He studied all kinds of painters and techniques. Of course, he had even met many of them throughout his life.

Now he was becoming quite popular in the online age, or rather, his art was becoming popular. He kept his face out of view of the public, and during exhibits, he always wore a mask. Keeping his face hidden was absolutely crucial.

However, one day he knew that he was bound to run into vampire hunters even despite his precautions.

The guests began to enter the building, and Pierre put on a colorful Italian mask and went downstairs to greet everyone.

The first person who approached him was of no surprise. It was a woman with long curly black hair named Margaret. She was obsessed with him.

In books, vampires are described

as stalkers, yet in complete opposition to the stories, Margaret was his stalker.

There were nights during which Pierre considered killing her. Also, shamefully, there was a moment when he wished she'd be the serial killer's next victim.

She fell into his arms and hugged him tightly. "This is so exciting! Such a privilege! So amazing! The most talented painter in the world living right here! I feel so special!"

Pierre nodded slightly and smiled. "Thank you, Margaret. As always, your enthusiasm outdoes anyone else's."

She put her lips to his ear. "Maybe tonight you'll finally show me your most private collection, with just the two of us there."

Pierre's mouth twisted in revulsion. *Maybe tonight I'll finally have the courage to kill you,* he thought, and sighed.

The turnout shocked him. The large gallery was absolutely packed. The catering staff had their work cut out for them. However, he did notice that most people were there for the free fancy food and drinks, not the art. Typical human behavior.

Margaret didn't let Pierre leave her sight the entire night. Closer to the end of the exhibit, Usseti walked through the doors. He, of course, wore a white suit, always in white. He had an expression of disdain as he watched others drinking wine and beer and eating sweets. Yet, his face lit up once he began to look at Pierre's paintings. He approached Pierre.

"My dear genius. Your art is outstanding. You know, I am an artist myself."

"Really?" Pierre answered.

Usseti wore a thin smile. "It's an art like no other; not everyone can understand it."

Pierre was a vampire, yet he felt chills run down his spine. Unlike everyone else in the room, he knew who Usseti actually was, and he understood what type of "art" he was talking about.

"Why don't they understand it, Usseti?"

"Because they have constricting beliefs."

"How so?"

Usseti merely smiled and continued observing the paintings. He was so careful, not a single wrong word to expose himself. Pierre was disgusted by him. He hated him, yet he held himself back. Many years ago, he had sworn not to get involved in such things.

He had ended a serial killer back home in France. The two sons of that man had assumed it was someone else who had done it. They slaughtered a whole family and then went on a rampage of vengeance. Children died because Pierre had taken justice into his own hands.

He understood his mistake. He was no divine figure, and he asked forgiveness from God and swore to never try to change things in the human community in such a way again. They had to figure out their disputes on their own — to follow their laws and rules, not the rules of a vampire.

What were his rules, anyway?

Pierre was so caught up in his own thoughts that he didn't notice everyone had left until he stood alone with Margaret.

"Pierre, you look surprised. I told the servants that you asked me to stay," she giggled. "Don't be mad at them."

"Margaret, you have to go. I need to think about a few things."

"I know who you are," she said,

slyly.

"What?"

Margaret took out a photo. He came closer to her. It was a picture of him.

"How?" He took off his mask since there was no point in keeping it on now.

"I have a night vision, long-range camera. I took this of you by your window."

Pierre closed his eyes. "Do you have more?"

"Just this one for now, but…I could easily post it online."

"No. You can't."

Suddenly her dress slid to the floor, and she stood there, naked.

"Show me your private collection upstairs, Pierre," Margaret said, seductively.

Pierre knew it had to be one of those rare times he would kill a human again.

However, he didn't feel as sad as he thought he would.

CHAPTER 7
LEND ME YOUR EARS

My name is Usseti, simply…Usetti. I
like to live a simple life…a peaceful life,
in this peaceful town. In the morning,
when I wake up, I love to watch the rays
of the beautiful sun peeking through
the window. I take my time because it's
not good to get up too fast. I follow the
same routine every morning. I must keep
my mind sharp and my body healthy. I
take a quick cold shower. Then I get to
my wonderful juicer and prepare freshly

squeezed celery juice. I drink 16 ounces because that's what clears the organs fully.

After, I go on a quick run. When I come back, of course, I shower again, and then I place horse placenta cream on my face. I must keep my skin young. Then comes the time for my breakfast. It usually consists of broccoli, spinach, carrots, cucumbers, and almonds. I despise meat...I despise meat eaters. Who in their right mind would want to live like that? And the coffee drinkers are even worse, the addicts.

Anyway, I like to prepare a second celery juice together with my breakfast. It gives me the strength I need for the day. Once my breakfast is finished, I go to the couch by the window and get ready for my favorite activity of the day, which is viewing my magnificent collection. Tenderly and with love, I take the large leather book with no title and slowly open it up. There, on every page, there is an ear sewn in, with a name under each one. I gently touch each ear. Every one of them is a memory. Yes, this is art, and I'm a special artist...perhaps even better and more talented than Pierre.

I shut my book after I'm fully satisfied, and at that point, I am prepared for the rest of my day. A large portion of it I spend observing others, of course; as you may know, I used to have a wonderful lunch spot, but for the time being, I have to settle for a different one in town. I bring my meal to a small table that's right in the center of this town. There I observe, and it's actually not so bad. Often I make mental notes regarding who I'd like to become part of my collection. I also make sure to be a gentleman, always opening the doors for the ladies and the elderly with a smile. I wave at the passersby and even give some money to the beggar at times. I have a good image in this town even though I rarely speak much to anybody.

On this day, just like any other day, I am observing townsfolk. I sit, watch and wonder what goes through their minds as they go about their daily routines. Some of them have their faces buried in their mobile phones. Awareness of their surroundings is completely gone. Perhaps that is why it's been so easy and simple for me to be an artist here. In another place, it might have been difficult, but not here, not in this peaceful town.

There goes investigator Pirel. He nods to me, and I smile back. The man has no clue. He thinks there are five murders to solve, but actually, there have already been ten. You see, I do not dispose of everybody the same way. Why would the authorities assume that? The town has had about 15 people go missing in the past year. Ten of them were my art projects, and the other five—well, I have no idea. Perhaps they are runaways, or maybe someone else got them, someone who'd just had enough. I don't honestly know why anyone would want to leave this peaceful town. I see some people are strange....

OOOH! Damn it! My white jacket! There's something on the sleeve! How? No, no, no! Don't tell me this is tomato! I knew I should not have packed tomatoes today. This is so frustrating. I can't believe it. Well, I feel sweat coming on my forehead. I know my face must be looking nervous right now. I quickly look around, checking to see if anyone is watching. No one's noticed yet! Frantically, with my hands shaking, I pack up the rest of my meal and walk home. I hate it when this happens. I must go and change my suit immediately and dump this one. I don't want to wash it. It won't be perfect again! I'll just skip eating tomatoes for a week. It's very maddening. Once I'm done with that, I'll be ready to go out once again; I have a few plans for the day.

***

At the same time, on the other side of town, Pirel was pondering the murders. He wasn't as clueless as Usseti assumed.

Pirel had had a special sense since childhood. He had never failed to solve a case, and he refused this one to be an exception. He felt badly for the victims and their families because the investigation was taking so long.

Today his senses led him back to one of the old homes on the outskirts of the community, one which had belonged to the young man who was the most recent victim.

Pirel stepped onto the old wooden, creaky porch. There was yellow tape blocking the way, but he simply slipped under the tape and unlocked the door.

An old feeling came over him, something he hadn't sensed in a long time. He felt woozy and nearly fell over. Pirel found a chair and sat down.

The scent.... He remembered telling others as a child about the scent, but no one else could smell it. Every time this happened, he met them.

The spirits of the departed sometimes were trapped in the physical world, perhaps because of trauma they couldn't get over. Sometimes they remained because of addiction. But many times, they stayed because of unfinished business. Was there one in this house right now?

Pirel suddenly felt chills and a hint of fear. When he was a kid, they'd never scared him, so why now?

He slowly got up and began walking towards the kitchen. As he got closer to the dining room, the feeling intensified.

He swallowed uneasily, took a deep breath and stepped into the room. There he was, at the window. The young man who had been killed recently.

He turned to Pirel, who sat down at the table not far from the ghost.

"I am glad you stopped by, dear investigator."

"Why are you still here?" Pirel queried.

"I am hoping to see."

"See what?"

"The end of the killings in this town," the ghost replied.

"Do you know who the killer is?"

"Sadly, I did not see his face, he was too far away, and then my heart stopped. The next moment I was here, in the house."

Pirel frowned in concentration. "He was far away when your heart stopped? You didn't see anything horrifying before your death?"

"No...I was out on a walk in the forest. I was quite happy."

Pirel leaned back in the chair, thinking. "From a distance.... I just don't get it."

The ghost watched Pirel carefully. "I have a feeling that you'll figure it out, Mr. Pirel."

Pirel nodded; he had to.

***

The day was rushing to its conclusion. The sun was starting to set over the town, and Usseti was finishing his dinner, preparing to go out for his long nighttime walk around the neighborhood. Sometimes he was very fortunate to find a new project during these walks.

The walking path began right by the main road. It was the busiest thoroughfare in town, but nothing compared to actual big city streets or even city suburbs. All it meant was that a car passed by every 30 seconds or more, and as it got darker, the cars became even less frequent.

On the other side of the path were tall bushes, some trees and old-style townhomes. Usseti preferred not to dwell on these too long, as the light was still too bright.

He reached the traffic lights of a crossroads and patiently waited. The sun had set. Across the road was the quietest suburban neighborhood in town. It was an atmosphere in which he was able to gather his thoughts best and come up with perfect plans and new projects.

This town was just too perfect for him. Usseti smiled as the light for the cars turned red, and he strode with pride into the street in front of the few cars that were waiting. Surely these were miserable people. They all only wished to be as free and fortunate as he. Those were his thoughts on the matter, at least.

This street had exceptionally fresh air, and each home was more beautiful than the next, all old-style architecture. The residences had large yards and a decent amount of space between each other. About every fifty meters stood a tall black streetlamp. All of them were rather dim; this was intentional so as not to bother the residents too much at night. It also made the street look more charming.

Usseti stopped each time he reached one of them and looked up at the light. From time to time, he'd meet one of the residents walking a dog. This night it was an old man with a poodle.

Usseti smiled at them, but the dog looked terrified. Dogs did not like Usseti. They sensed his aura…the hidden bloodlust, the devastating urge.

When Usseti had to wait to kill, he often became frantic. It would eat him up inside. At times he'd find himself pressing his fingertips against a window, scratching his head until it was painful, ripping the skin off his toes. For him, imagining things only made his compulsion worse, and he'd sweat about not being able to actually give in to it.

"I simply must continue to create," muttered Usseti to himself as he reached the end of the path.

Before him was a little pond with a small garden to the side. Usseti liked to take a break there on a bench, under cover of total darkness. He always hoped that he'd find some lonely unfortunate soul wandering there.

This night, sadly, his wish was granted. A man who just had a fight with his family had stormed out of his house and went to smoke alone by the lake. Usseti rose to his feet, his heartbeat elevated, his pupils dilated, his skin burning with excitement. He reached inside his suit.

A minute later, the man was lying dead, hidden in thick bushes, his blood slowly creating a tiny stream that led into the pond. It was coming from the side of his head — the spot where his left ear had once been attached.

CHAPTER 8
DON'T VISIT AT NIGHT

It was a rainy day in Gravil, which didn't seem to match what was going on at all. An Egyptian exhibit had come into town, and the Main Street Museum had been cleared for the exhibit. The crowd was enthusiastically lining up to enter, even in the rain.

Among those was the Mirrel family, who owned a café. There were a father, a mother and a boy. The boy was very observant and full of questions.

"Why aren't they letting everyone in faster? It's raining!"

His father snorted. "Good question, son. It's incompetence."

"What's that?"

"Not doing a proper job."

Finally, the doors opened, and the family entered. The first things the boy noticed were four black dog statues.

"These look alive."

"They are Egyptian dogs, just statues, son," said his mother.

He wasn't so convinced, as he was certain that one of the dogs had glanced at him for an instant.

"Son, come on."

In a glass case were some golden artifacts and ancient jewelry. Right outside of it was a group of men standing close to each other and whispering. The boy thought this was very suspicious as well.

"What's wrong with those men? Why are they all close like that and whispering?"

"Boy, hush! They'll hear you. They are just trying to be polite. Enjoy your experience. Don't worry about others," the mother remonstrated.

Little did the parents know that the boy's observations were correct.

Night came, and the museum was closed, but not everyone went home. The men whom the boy had noticed were back but now in black masks, hiding in the shrubs behind the building, checking the area.

They just needed that weirdo in the white suit to stop pacing in front of the building. It was getting late.

"What's with this guy?" one of the men said to his companions. "He's just whispering to himself, walking back and forth."

It was indeed a strange night for Usetti, as the local market had run out of his favorite salad mix, the one he liked to eat on Friday nights. It was outrageous, and he just couldn't calm down.

The men waited another half an hour, and finally, Usseti left. They made their move towards a window they had tampered with earlier.

There were four of them. After one had nimbly gotten inside the window, the biggest one struggled to get in, even with his two compatriots pushed and the first man pulled from inside the museum. After much huffing and puffing, all four robbers were inside. With their bags in hand, they went straight toward the section they had observed earlier.

Suddenly they heard a sound from the long wide hallway. Heavy, quick steps were approaching. They all froze, standing in the shadows.

Out of the darkness, onto the floor, lit up by glorious moonlit coming from a skylight, emerged a large black dog. Its eyes were green, and it looked directly at them.

"What the hell is that…?"

The dog growled as it bent its legs back. Three more dogs of the same kind appeared from behind the first one.

"Ruuuun!" yelled the big guy as they frantically scattered in different directions. The dogs split up, chasing each man.

The largest man found an office, ducked inside, and quickly locked the door. He heard terrifying screams from down the hall. The dogs had caught two of the robbers and tore them apart. The other one, still alive, hid in the men's restroom and sat in a stall, shaking. The screams stopped very quickly.

The dogs consumed the bodies,

leaving absolutely nothing, not even a drop of blood or a tiny bone. It was as if those men had never existed.

The large man was breathing heavily behind a desk in the office, afraid but certain the dogs could not get him there. But he couldn't have been more wrong. The door came down with a violent bang. He couldn't even scream as his heart seized violently, and he died from the myocardial infarction. It was better than being eaten alive.

Meanwhile, the last burglar got the courage to come out of the stall and was trying to open the window of the restroom. It took him a few minutes, but he finally succeeded. With relief and pure joy as he lifted himself up onto the sill and was about to jump down.

He celebrated too soon. One of the dogs grabbed his ankle and swiftly pulled him back inside.

In the morning, when the museum reopened, the manager was shocked to see the door to his office broken. Yet nothing in the museum was missing. It was a mystery....

And Usseti finally got his salad....

CHAPTER 9
THE BOSS WANTS A PAINTING

The mob boss stretched out his short legs. He was still fuming about his daughter and her boyfriend. Were girls even supposed to date at age 16?

He had the young man over for dinner and said a bunch of subtly creepy things, but the guy was clearly too dumb to understand the dark jokes and hints. The young ignorant moose just kept smiling all night as though his lips were stapled to his upper cheeks. The boss couldn't even stand thinking about his face. His rictus grin made him look like the damn Joker from the Batman movies.

As the boss browsed various art pieces on his computer tablet while contemplating these things, he saw a gorgeous painting of an old French village. However, it wasn't for sale; in fact, it was a portal to the artist's page. He opened it. Pierre?

He had a huge following!

The boss almost spilled his whiskey as he grabbed the edge of his desk. Thirty million followers?

Who was this guy? In Gravil? Humph. That's so close. He even had a business there! The boss clicked on the profile.

The artist wore a mask in his photo. What was that about? He tried to find out what this guy looked like. Nothing. No family history, no face, no personal history. Just that he lived and worked in Gravil.

The boss called in a few of his men. A thin short guy named Roberto was in the lead.

"Roberto, I got a task for you and the boys. Go to Gravil and find a painter named Pierre. I'll send you a screenshot of the painting I want. Pay whatever he wants. Even if it's millions."

Roberto and two others immediately went downstairs and got into the Aston Martin. They were off to Gravil.

***

It was a huge contrast driving from the city to Gravil. As they got closer, the air was much better, and they rolled down the windows. Roberto loved coming to these parts. Mountains, lakes, rivers, forests, vast green fields. It was a paradise.

They got to Gravil at about midday

and parked in front of a health food grocery store. Right outside of it sat a slim, tall man in an all-white outfit. Roberto approached him.

"Hey, you, where does a painter named Pierre live?"

Usetti stared at Roberto coldly. He hated when anyone addressed him impolitely, especially if he was an outsider.

The icy gaze made Roberto feel uneasy as he felt his left hand beginning to slightly shake. Immediately he was contrite. "I'm sorry, sir; I don't mean to disturb you. I just really need to locate this artist."

Now Usseti was mollified. He slowly raised his finger and leaned back. "Pierre only sees interested parties at night, so you'll have to wait. His red mansion is located in the western area of the town…you can't miss it."

"Only at night?"

"Correct."

"Why?"

Usseti gazed haughtily at the man. "Am I he? How should I know? Privacy, perhaps? Maybe he's a vampire!" Usseti laughed at his own joke as Roberto thanked him and got back into the car.

"That is one creepy weirdo. I got some strange vibes from him," said Roberto to the other two. They headed towards the mansion.

Finding it wasn't an issue. When they met the butler, it was indeed confirmed that they could only meet Pierre after nine o'clock that night. They were invited into a small guest house to wait. There, servants brought them coffee, croissants and fresh bread with butter. The men were more than happy to relax and wait. The hours dragged on slowly, but finally, the butler came in to fetch them.

They entered the mansion and were asked to sit on a couch near an antique fireplace.

A few minutes after they sat down, a voice came from behind them. They were all startled and quickly turned around. A man in all black, wearing a colorful mask, walked around and sat in an upholstered chair across from them.

"Greetings, gentlemen. I hear you are interested in an art purchase?"

"Yes, sir, for our boss. Here is what he wants." Roberto showed Pierre the photo of the painting. Pierre shook his head.

"That one is not for sale."

"How about a print?"

"I don't do prints or copies. I sell only originals, yet that one is not for sale." He pointed up at a wall above a spiral staircase. The beautiful, enchanting painting of his home village hung there. Roberto's breath was taken away. How could someone paint like that?

"The boss will pay anything. Millions if necessary."

"I have a vast amount of money, gentlemen. It's not for sale. I'm sorry." He got up and walked towards the steps. "The butler will see you out."

Roberto was angry. Once outside the house, he stood by the car with the other two. "We will get a hotel room nearby and come back tomorrow during the day to take it. The boss won't take no for an answer."

Pierre watched from a dark window upstairs and heard every word.

As the men drove towards the grand hotel located at the edge of the town, Pierre swiftly flew to the car and damaged the tires. The Aston Martin spun to the side of the road into a ditch.

Pierre stayed to make sure no one was dead but also to hear what they'd say. The hotel was still four miles away.

Roberto called the boss, and that man sounded furious on the phone. He told them to walk to the hotel and that he was sending another car with several more men.

As Roberto and the two sidekicks gloomily dragged their feet toward the hotel, Pierre flew to meet the other car.

Pierre hadn't had so much fun in a while. He laughed to himself when he heard the driver of the second car calling the boss. Yet, that man was stubborn. He said he would come down on his own in the morning. It was time for Pierre to get a bit rougher.

He knew the location of the mob boss' luxurious villa, and he arrived there quite swiftly. He examined the home and made sure no one was there. Then he set the villa on fire.

The boss was in shock seeing his home ablaze when he arrived later. He dropped to his knees and decided that pursuing the art brought him bad luck.

The boss gave up on the painting, and Pierre had his fun. A win-win for the French master of art.

Good night, Gravil. Usseti is in bed early tonight, so enjoy this moment.

CHAPTER 10
THE CROW

Shiny tiny things.

The large crow living in Gravil loved to collect those. He did not steal them, oh no. If someone left them outside, it meant they didn't care, and that's when he'd swoop down and collect. He was a kind crow—patient, wise.

Yet, there was one thing that drove him really crazy, and that was when anyone stole one of his shiny things. Such a bad situation had arisen on this particular morning as he was flying around and looking for something new to add to his collection. Below he saw the house of another collector, a human with a very nasty aura. The crow saw a very nice shiny thing lying on the backyard table, but the man was sitting there, eating. The crow had to land on a branch and wait patiently.

Usseti was eating an avocado salad. He noticed the abnormally large crow land on the branch not far from him. The bird was staring at the table.

"How odd. What is with this bird?" Usseti muttered to himself. He decided to observe from inside the house once he finished his food. He went in and watched from the window.

The big crow landed on the table.

"Wait! My watch! My father's watch! I forgot it there!"

Usseti rushed outside, but the bird

was already in the air with the watch in its beak. Usseti started running through the forest, trying to follow its flight.

"Damn it, damn it!" Usseti was so busy watching the crow he didn't notice his perfect white suit getting dirty and damaged. Perhaps the watch was important to him, indeed.

The crow reached the foothills of the mountains and alighted on the top of a tall rock formation.

The crow had built a nest there and was collecting all kinds of shiny things in the nest. He wondered why that crazy human was following him. That man had left this shiny thing alone, so he did not want it.

Meanwhile, Usseti was climbing the rocks like a possessed madman. His breathing was frantic, he had torn parts of his white suit, yet he was desperate to get that watch back.

The crow saw the man getting closer, and as usual, when faced with a thief, he became enraged. The crow flew up, circled around and began to attack the man, striking him on the head, neck, and back.

Usseti was in shock. He could barely hold on, and then he lost his grip and fell.

Luck was truly on his side as he landed on several bushes, which cushioned his fall. Usseti saw the crow flying down towards him. He reached into his suit.

"I guess there is a first for everything." A moment later, the crow lay dead on the ground. Its heart had stopped. Bloodied up, Usseti again climbed the rock outcropping, found his watch in the nest, and stumbled back home.

However, the town drunk, Dan,

had seen the entire episode from his seat at the bottom of a tree several yards away.

Later on, when he sobered up, Dan had no clue whether what he had seen was real or not, so did it even matter in the end?

CHAPTER 11

NOT SO JELLO

The Mirrel café on the far eastern side of town had been open for fifteen years. It had become one of the most popular destinations in town for locals and travelers alike.

The Mirrel family consisted of a father, a mother and a son. The café specialized in gelatin desserts and coffee. However, they also served freshly squeezed juice.

Its unique atmosphere and delicious

treats made it a place impossible to resist for everyone who tried it. People always went back. Some favorites from the menu were Thick Dark Chocolate Jello, White and Black Jello, House Coffee, Gravil Mocha, and Orange/Cherry Juice.

The décor also was unique. Each table had an aquarium placed next to it. The beautiful, clear water was filled with colorful fish, and the patrons enjoyed watching the fish as they waited for their orders.

The family house was attached to the café, and this made it easier to keep everything running perfectly, but it still was a ton of work.

One particular day, things were going as usual. However, the Mirrel family was about to get a few uncommon visitors.

Several tables were occupied. Mom and Dad were busy making the food while the boy served as the waiter. Dad always had the local radio on quietly. He did not want to disturb the customers, so it was just loud enough for him to hear it.

"A fugitive has escaped the high-security prison in Darbingham and was last seen running into the Moriquette forest."

Dad looked over at Mom, who was getting one of the Dark Chocolate Jello specials ready. She looked as good as ever, and he loved watching her. Mom glanced back and caught his eyes looking below her waist. She smiled and laughed. "Keep that for tonight."

He laughed and then pointed at the radio. "You hear that about the criminal? That's close to Gravil."

"With all that's been happening here, I wouldn't be surprised if he was already in Gravil."

As she said it, the bell over the door

rang. They both immediately looked to see who'd come in and were relieved to see the man in the everlasting white suit, Usseti, who came in twice a month for some Orange/Cherry juice. He slowly approached the counter and greeted them. They already knew what he'd request.

"A seat at the far left side by the window, and the Orange/Cherry, is that right, Mr. Usseti?" Mr. Mirrel asked.

Usseti smiled. "Wonderful service, as usual."

He followed the boy to his favorite table. On the way, he glanced at a couple enjoying coffee and gelatin.

Bastards. They're sick, he thought as he sat down and gazed at the street outside. If he hadn't liked this juice so much, he'd never come into this café. He couldn't stand seeing people consume coffee and sugar.

Suddenly a man in a ragged brown jacket came into Usseti's view, running towards the café. He was unshaven, looking like a nasty barbarian. He had his hand inside the jacket.

Don't tell me this Mr. Nasty is coming here too, Usseti thought as he sipped his juice.

But the man did come crashing into the door. Things were about to get very interesting for the Mirrel family.

Sweating and looking frantic, the man stumbled across the room and sat at a table in a dark corner. The boy approached to bring him a cup of water. But suddenly, sirens could be heard coming toward the building. The man grabbed the boy, pulling him into the booth seat and then took out a gun, holding it against the boy's head.

The parents and all the patrons except Usseti were paralyzed with fear.

The mother, however, overcame her initial shock and wracked her brain as to how she could help her son.

She took a deep breath, and from where she stood, she said, "Sir, I'll go out and tell the police not to enter. That's my son there. Please don't hurt him. We will cooperate."

The man nodded. "Go, tell the police that people will die if they come in here. Tell them I need a car, a fast car, with a full tank of gas. Now!"

She nodded and went outside. She met Pirel there and explained the situation. Then she went back inside. "They'll do as you say, but please don't take my son with you."

"I'll go in his place when the car is ready," said the father.

The man nodded. He took a sip of water. He looked as though he were starving.

"Sir. We are famous for our treats here. You look like you could use some food. Can I please offer you our best chocolate Jello?" offered Mrs. Mirrel.

Usseti smirked. Could it be that this woman had thought of exactly what he wanted to see?

The criminal hesitated but then nodded in agreement.

The woman smiled. "Coming right up." She bustled into the kitchen. She was not a killer, but the only thing she had available to stop the criminal was rat poison.

So she mixed it into the thick, viscous gelatin. When it was ready, she took it to the table, careful to keep a neutral look on her face. She gently put it down in front of the man and backed away, staying a few meters away.

The man began to eat with one free hand. "Wow, this is very good!" He sped up the pace, gobbling it all down quickly. Before he could say more, he began to convulse.

The mother flew into action and grabbed her son, shoving him into the kitchen. The criminal aimed his gun at her, but he was unable to focus and only got off a few useless shots. The patrons panicked and ran towards the door.

They had nothing to fear. The criminal fell on the floor, and gradually the convulsions stopped, and his eyes rolled back into their sockets. It was over.

The family had run out the door too, and the only one who remained seated inside was Usseti. He calmly finished drinking his juice through a straw and shook his head, smiling.

CHAPTER 12
DON'T LOOK

There was a reason why after serving as an assassin, Usseti had come to live in the small town of Gravil.

It wasn't just the fact that it was a peaceful town surrounded by beautiful scenery, which was great for a health enthusiast.

On the far north outskirts of the town stood an old abandoned house. Usseti had no interest in the dwelling, but it was the very house he was born in.

When he was only five years old, Usseti learned that his father had killed many people and that their bodies were hidden in the walls and floors of the house. But in the end, he was caught.

Just before he died, his father gave young Usseti his watch, and before the authorities arrived, the five-year-old was taken away by his uncle, a gang leader who later died of a drug overdose when Usseti was 14. Since then, Usseti had lived on his own.

But let's go back to that house, to the time of the police raid.

When the police arrived, led by Pirel's father, Jean, something even more horrific had entered the house: a dark spirit of incredible power. In the fight that ensued, Usseti's father was killed, and so were most of the policemen. But the killings were not just from bullets. Jean barely got away, and he told everyone of a shadow creature that killed anyone who laid eyes upon it. He felt fortunate to have fallen out of the window and suffered only a broken leg.

Later, Jean and the other officers were able to investigate the house during the day, but no one would go there at night. Many years passed, and the story of the evil shadow became a legend that was known by everyone in town.

Yet, a couple of stupid teenagers wanted to test it out, and that is why Pirel found himself there one morning in the same spot his father had stood many years before. The teens' bikes were outside the house, and Pirel feared the worst.

He slowly entered the old creaky building. The stench of death…He knew it right away, and being sensitive to spirits, he also felt the immense evil. Pirel fought back nausea, and his knees began to ache.

The legend stated that anyone who looked at the thing died, but it only came out at night.

Pirel found fresh blood in one of the old ruined rooms. The kids were dead, all right. He went outside and sat on an old bench to think.

"From where does it emerge?" he murmured to himself.

"From a demonic portal."

Pirel quickly turned toward the voice. There stood a man he knew well, a church minister named Dalk, who was blind.

"Pastor! What are you doing here? You walked all this way?"

"Indeed, young man. We can no longer ignore this evil, for it has hurt us again. You must help me prepare the house, my young friend."

"How?" Pirel was taken aback.

"That thing cannot stand any form of light, yet it is bound to this house. If we make it impossible for it to escape light when the portal opens, it'll be gone or destroyed."

Pirel thought a moment. "Why don't we just burn the house down?"

The minister shook his head. "Many have tried that already. It doesn't burn."

"Why do you think your plan will work?"

"I only know that we must try. That is all."

Pirel's mouth was set in a thin line. "What do I have to do?"

"Go buy lamps that run on batteries and many candles. Bring any police officers brave enough to set it all up."

They labored for hours getting the house ready. As twilight approached, everyone left the house except for Dalk.

Every hallway and every room had candles, flashlights and lamps all over. There were no shadows to be seen. The only room that was dark was the one that Dalk sat in. He had something in his hand as he patiently waited in the middle of the floor.

Then the blind minister heard it, a strange sound right next to his ear. A whisper in an unknown language and what sounded like the scratching of claws on the floor. The heavy breathing was right against his face. The scratching intensified.

"You must be upset that I am blind. You must see the eyes to kill. Well, let me show you better."

Pastor pressed a button in his hand, and the whole room lit up with lights and lamps. He heard a horrific scream and then a crashing on the floor. A few more seconds passed, and he smelled something burning. The monster's flesh was on fire. The house's curse was broken, and it all went up in flames.

Though Pirel and his men rushed toward the flames and firefighters tried to enter, they were not able to save Dalk. The man sacrificed himself to rid the town of that evil.

Pirel walked alone along the cobblestone street leading to his house. The high dim street lamps provided just enough light. He considered Dalk's determination to root out the evil.

Somewhere in this town, among these good, peaceful people, lived a terrible killer. Someone who destroyed lives. How many families had said their last goodbyes to daughters, sons, spouses, and parents, without realizing it? He had to root this evil out as well, just as Dalk had. No matter the price.

CHAPTER 13
THE WRITER

In the dark night, I sit by the window. The pen in my hand is like a magical tool of creation. I sit and observe the outside world. The candlelight is all I need. This small thing stirs my imagination.

For so many years, I have created dark characters. I achieved fame and fortune and perhaps became a dark character myself.

I went insane and did shameful things…but then I moved to a quiet town named Gravil.

Here in this peaceful place, living alone and hiding from everyone, I thought that I was through with darkness. Yet, ironically, it was in this town that my darkest creation became alive.

When the news broke of a serial killer in town, I was angry. I felt as though fate were against me, crushing me. Then, my mind took a turn, and as I began writing again, I changed my opinion.

I was creating the darkest character yet. My own serial killer.

On one not so special occasion, I sat on a street bench in the middle of the day. Suddenly I noticed a man in an all-white suit standing by a tree, surreptitiously watching someone from behind it. He was tall, thin, and handsome.

It was this man I chose to represent the killer in my book. Perhaps it wasn't fair to this fellow, so I had my character wear a purple suit instead.

Whenever I saw this man around town, I made sure to follow him like a stalker. I watched what he ate, drank… his manners.

The more I followed him, the more I realized that this was a very strange man. Not that I wasn't! But I was starting to actually suspect him of nefarious deeds.

One evening I followed him through an alleyway. When I emerged from it, I suddenly felt tremendous pain in my chest. I collapsed, but luckily someone had seen me, and I was quickly taken to a hospital. Miraculously I survived the heart attack, but for some reason, my legs became paralyzed.

Hmph. Quite a dark twist of fate.

So, now I sit by my window at night, imagining things that the killer is doing. The killer who looks just like that young man.

CHAPTER 14
WHAT COMES AROUND

The mob boss knew about his competitors in and around Gravil. He owned a farm there, but the local farmers were beating him out of the market. The farm only represented about one percent of his income, so it wasn't a huge monetary loss, but his greed and pride drove his anger.

He already resented the place because of the incident with the painting. Pierre, that weird masked freak! He threw his glass of whiskey at the wall. It broke, and when his servant went to clean up the glass, he cut himself. The boss looked at him with fiery eyes.

"You moron, you gonna bleed on my carpet!? It's worth more than you!"

The man ran out of the room, terrified. The boss called for his advisor, who was there in a minute.

"I can't take this no more. That joker boyfriend of my daughter is driving me crazy. Then that painter, the freak. Now the farm? I'm having a breakdown."

The other man's face was impassive. "What does your heart tell you about the farm, sir?"

The boss sat quietly for a moment, and then an evil smile appeared on his face. He waved his arm. "Gather the men. We will burn the competitors out."

Sadly, the boss proceeded with this devious plan, and fires were started around several farms in the area. The air was thick and fog-like, and ash rained down. The people in town could smell the burnt wood as some of the fires spread to the forest. The firefighters came in large numbers from all the nearby towns and the city. They battled hard and eventually put them out, but the damage to the farms was huge.

Satisfied, the boss made plans to return to the city. But before he did that, he decided to spend some time by the lake. He ordered his bodyguards to stay by the cars since he didn't want those oafs disturbing his peace and quiet.

The boss made his way along the trail to the beautiful, still lake. He sat on a large rock and took out some food. Salami, coffee in a thermos, bread.

From behind a tree, he was watched by a man who despised those things, but this man was ecstatic at the sight of another person alone in the forest, totally unsuspecting.

Usseti had just killed another victim earlier this morning on the other side of this forest. How fortunate was it that he was able to collect two in one day! *Two for the price of one*, he thought. He stood not too far behind the boss, smiling.

A few minutes later, the boss was lying motionless over his food. His left ear was missing. Blood dripped on the salami.

Usseti almost skipped home. His heart was full of joy. The madman's collection was growing. But today, he'd actually done a lot of people a great favor. He wouldn't have been happy to know that.

CHAPTER 15
GIANT ISSUES

For the longest time, going up into the mountains near Gravil has been considered a bad idea. There were many rumors flying around about all kinds of dangers.

However, this didn't seem to stop the Mirrel family. The father was insistent that the only people who had gotten in trouble were those who went alone. He convinced his wife, and then his son knew he'd have to go along, though he was the one who resisted the most. Unfortunately, his parents did not trust the child's instincts; they had no idea how right he'd been about the museum trouble or that he saw a dark aura around Usseti. The boy knew it was pointless to argue, as his parents would only say something like, "You're not getting enough sleep," or "It's just your imagination."

So one fine day, they headed up the mountains, and at midday, they stopped to look for a perfect spot to set up their picnic.

After some time searching, they found a grassy meadow with a few bushes. It was a very warm and clear day. The slight breeze made the experience feel almost perfect.

Mr. Mirrel had a look of extreme satisfaction on his face. He stretched out his hand to emphasize the beauty of the view below. They could see the whole town, fields, the lake and the forest. The birds were singing.

A bit sullenly, the boy sat on the corner of the blanket, eating round golden crackers and sliced apples. His parents were enjoying some light beers and cheese croissants.

However, about twenty minutes into the picnic, the family heard heavy footsteps coming toward them. As they turned toward the sound, an incredibly tall and large man with a deformed face suddenly towered over them. A moment later, another one, slightly shorter, joined him. Before they could move or scream, the giants picked them up and carried them away. They hollered for help but to no avail. The giants were carrying them farther into the mountains, away from the town.

Eventually, they entered a thick

wooded area. As the giants stopped, the family saw a long wooden house and large wooden cages next to it. The giants placed the family in one of the cages. The big one grunted, "You won't be in there long. Tomorrow morning, you'll be our breakfast!" He gave a guttural laugh and stalked away.

The poor terrified boy sat in the corner, watching his mom and dad. If only they had listened to him. The parents tried to remain calm and think of a solution. But all they could do was pray.

As night drew near, the boy sat with his mother's arms encircling him. Both had tears in their eyes. As they waited for their fate to unfold, the bushes rustled. A child came out, but this child was the size of an adult human male. He came close to the cage and looked at the boy.

"You are a kid, like me?"

The boy went to the bars of the cage.

"Yes, I am," he answered. "How old are you?"

"I am six."

"Me too."

"You look so sad. Are you crying?"

"Yes, your family wants to eat us."

The giant boy was quiet for a moment. He lowered his head, thinking. Then he looked up with a smile.

"Do you want to be friends? There are no other kids around here, ever."

"Yes." With that, the boy took a small rubber ball out of his pocket and showed the giant how it bounced. The giant boy laughed.

"As a new friend, I'd like to give this to you, but in return, as a gift, you have to let us out. So this way, we can play again in the future."

The giant boy thought for a moment again. The parents held their breath. Then the boy went to the mechanism and unlocked the door. The human boy handed him the ball.

"We can play together when I return," he said with a smile.

The giant boy nodded and went back into the forest with his new toy.

The father lifted up his son, and together with the mother, they ran for their lives.

By the time they got back into town, both of the parents had bloodied feet and could barely stand, yet the only real hero of this event was the six-year-old boy who had saved his family.

From this point on, the Mirrel parents took their son's words more seriously. And the giant boy dreamed of his friend coming back. In his heart, he doubted they'd return, but he felt that letting them go had been the right thing to do.

CHAPTER 16
A FISHY SITUATION

Dan started out as a police officer and later became a detective. He was good at the job; there seemed to be no crime he could not solve.

Dan had a partner named Tom, who was an older detective. That man had taught him a lot of things, and because Dan's father died when he was young, Tom became a sort of father figure to him.

Dan married early, and his son

was already a teenager by the time Tom entered his final year of service. Tom was excited to finally retire. He told Dan that he'd go and live peacefully in Hawaii. Dan loved that idea, although he was sad that his mentor was retiring and he'd probably be given a new rookie partner.

However, on one dark night, Dan's whole life changed in an instant. Dan and Tom were investigating a drug dealing gang and found the leader to be mysterious and elusive. In hopes of uncovering who he was, they looked at lower-ranked members of the gang and for the users they supplied.

One night, a confidential informer on the street told them that a new member of the gang was selling at an old abandoned apartment complex. Tom and Dan surreptitiously headed into the complex.

Right away, they found two men

who ran in different directions. One darted down a hall, and the other ran up some stairs. Tom went after the one headed upstairs, and Dan ran after the guy who dashed down the hall.

Dan had trouble keeping up with the dealer, but he managed and finally got his perp cornered. He raised his gun and pointed at the guy, who stood in the shadows.

"Come into the light, now, show your hands."

The guy slowly came into view. Moonlight streamed through a window, illuminating his face. Dan was shocked. Cold sweat appeared on his forehead. It was his son's best friend, Jeremy.

"What are you doing here, Jeremy? My son better not be involved," Dan said, pointing his gun at the youth.

Jeremy was contrite. "No, sir. I swear, he has no idea. I'd never do that to him. I am desperate, sir. I'm sorry. Please let me go. I'll never do it again."

Dan hesitated. He debated whether to let the boy go or not. Prison would ruin the kid's life, but drugs ruined the lives of others as well. As Dan lost his focus and lowered his gun, Jeremy slowly reached behind himself and whipped out his own gun. At the moment Jeremy fired, someone pushed Dan out of the way. Dan hit the wall but kept his balance and shot Jeremy twice in the chest. Jeremy dropped the gun and collapsed. Dan quickly looked to see who had saved him. It was Tom, who was now lying on the floor with a head wound.

Dan knelt next to his partner and shook him. He sobbed and begged God for a miracle, but it was all over. Tom was dead.

Dan knew that the death of his best friend and his son's best friend were on him. It was his mistake. He resigned that very week. Thus began Dan's deep depression as he slid into alcoholism.

His wife, Mary and son, Rick, sold their city apartment and took Dan to live in a quiet, peaceful town called Gravil. Here they hoped to see him recover.

Yet, despite showing some signs of improvement, Dan found a couple of other drunks and often sneaked out to imbibe with them.

Today was just such a day. Dan had no idea that, once again, he would experience a powerful, life-changing moment.

Dan and his two alcoholic buddies, Leon and Darnell, decided it was a good idea to go fishing, despite it being on the brink of winter. It was almost freezing out.

But Dan was leery of going out on the water, especially in cold weather.

He made the excuse that he had strange nightmares about drowning. The two others laughed at him but agreed that he'd stay on the shore, watching them. They left Dan a six-pack of beers and took another one for themselves. They'd already downed a six-pack before they even got on the rowboat.

It was slightly foggy over the still lake, yet despite the chill, it was a nice enough day — nothing coats and alcohol couldn't fix! Leon and Darnell got the boat to the center of the lake, put out a finishing line, and started working on the beers. Dan leaned against a trunk of an old tree and watched them, already finishing his third beer.

He tipped the can toward the sky, suddenly melancholy. "Ahh, here's another one for you, Tom, old buddy." As Dan brought his eyes back to the lake, he thought he saw something moving in the water—moving in a way he had never seen before. If it were one large fish, it would make only a single wake line, but there were three lines moving as one. Then just for a split second, he thought he saw two tentacles break the water on each side of the center wake.

"What the…" Dan sat up, his eyes riveted on the water. Was he that out of it? Was he hallucinating now? Or had he actually seen something weird?

The two other drunks were having the time of their lives. They drank, laughed, and told each other absurd jokes. As Leon was finishing telling another one of these, the boat slightly rocked side to side as though something had pushed it from below.

"What's that? What the hell?" Darnell looked at Leon and shook his head.

Darnell guffawed. "Are you that

stupid, man? Nothing out here, just a big fish, buddy boy. Why you freaking out? Huh? You think…. AGHHHHHHH!"

A tentacle twisted around Darnell's right arm, and a large mouth with many rows of sharp teeth emerged from the water. Darnell screamed like a wild animal. Leon grabbed him and pulled him back.

SNAP!

Leon fell back, holding Darnell. "I got you, buddy. Let's row back!"

However, Darnell's screaming intensified as blood gushed everywhere. His right arm had been bitten off just below the elbow.

Dan stood up and began wobbling along the shore. He could hear his pals yelling, but what could he do? What was going on? He couldn't see clearly because of the fog.

Meanwhile, Leon turned the boat

around and was starting to row back. Sadly, his efforts were in vain. One of the oars was violently ripped away from him by two large tentacles and thrown far out into the water.

"No, no!" Leon raised the other oar and was hitting the water with it randomly, screaming in panic. Tentacles came up from behind him, wrapped around his waist and pulled him into the lake. A tiny pool of blood appeared where he had disappeared.

Darnell was now moaning in pain, barely conscious. As he lay in the boat, tentacles snaked up and took him under the water as well. The empty boat floated farther and farther away from the shore until Dan could no longer see it at all.

Did what had happened really happen? Had he truly seen a creature? Had he heard the screaming? Or had the other two just rowed farther out into the lake, looking for a better fishing spot?

Dan waited for hours, but the other men never came back. In shock and sober, he finally realized his denial of the state he was in.

That day Dan went home and apologized to his wife and son. He began the journey of sobriety. It was the one good thing that came out of that awful situation.

A week later, after several very tough days, Dan sat outside at a café. It was snowing lightly. He was drinking tea with lemon and having a salad with grilled chicken. He felt some of his old senses coming back as he noticed a man in an all-white suit observing a young woman in a red jacket who was eating alone. To Dan, it didn't look like a regular guy just checking out a girl. This man's eyes and mannerisms had not a single hint of lust or sexual drive. It was something else entirely. He had seen this look before when he was a detective, but where? The damage alcohol had done to his memory was tremendous.

Things got even more suspicious when the girl got up and left, and the man followed in the same direction just moments after. The day was quite cold; how could the guy run around in a summer suit? Perhaps the sinister behavior was just Dan's imagination or a hope that he was getting his old investigator's senses back. He couldn't be sure.

Yet, two days later, when this very same girl's body was found in the forest, Dan realized that he had to go to Pirel, even if he were wrong about the guy in white.

CHAPTER 17
MOTOR FROM HADES

A quiet night in the Gravil mountains was broken by the roaring engine of a powerful motorcycle. It did not sound like a normal bike, with someone just gunning it and showing off; instead, it sounded like a mix of thunder and a very loud engine. The birds flew away as it passed. Frogs hid under the leaves. Deer ran deep into the forest. Even the giants awakened, confused. Pierre stood on his balcony, as his sensitive ears could hear sounds from very far away.

The motorcycle was heading into town. As it drove through the outskirts, Usseti sat up in bed, feeling instant rage. The right amount of hours of sleep was essential to his well-being.

And, of course, as this sound spread through the main street, the police went into action. Two cars turned on their lights and were following the large black motorcycle. The rider was also all in black, with a red helmet. He pulled into a gas station but remained seated without killing the engine. As the police drove in, he tossed something at one of the gas pumps, and it instantly exploded into flames. The rider roared off down the road.

One of the police cars went after him, while the other stayed to help the gas station attendant and call the fire department.

The pursuing cop called for backup. All of the department's cars were out on the road now, with one setting up a blockade down the main road. The motorcycle was creating distance between himself and the police; his speed was abnormally fast. However, when he reached the blockade, he tried to go right through it and smashed into one of the police cars. The rider flew off the bike and flipped many times, hitting the road while the motorcycle itself slid into the field at the side.

The policeman rushed to the rider. Amazingly, he was able to get up, and just as he pulled out a gun, they subdued him and handcuffed him.

One officer pulled off the rider's helmet, revealing a crazed, frantic-looking face. As the policemen struggled to get him into their squad car, his demeanor changed. He was calm and cooperative, and he looked very confused.

The officers peppered the man with questions. He nearly sobbed, claiming the "cursed motorcycle controlled" his mind. Believing that he might be under the influence of illicit drugs, the police took him into custody.

But it was negligent of them to leave the motorcycle where it was. They called a towing company to impound it rather than take it in immediately.

The guy, Charles, in charge of the local business, was not the fastest man around. He took his sweet time to get up when the police called. He made tea, got a baguette and slowly spread the butter, then he calmly cut the salami. He was in no rush at all.

Meanwhile, a car full of teens made its way down the same road. They were coming back from a party.

Mike was a small guy who was often

bullied by the other guys. He constantly tried to fit in and please everyone. This only made things worse.

Tonight he was crammed against the back window when he saw something in the field next to the road. "Stop the car!"

"What? Don't tell me what to do, Mike," said the driver.

"Maybe the little bitch is gonna puke, man," said the muscular jock next to Mike. "I don't want that on me."

"Get him the hell out then!"

They slammed the brakes and pushed Mike out of the car.

"Do your business, little freak, but do it fast!" yelled the driver.

"No, you guys go," Mike said, nonchalantly. They laughed crazily and took off, glad to leave him stranded.

Mike walked towards the tall grass. There lay a black motorcycle. Mike's eyes seemed to burn red as the motorcycle whispered to him. He managed to get it upright and sat in the saddle. Immediately he felt as though he'd had years of experience riding it. With a wild scream, he took off after the guys in the car. As they laughed and joked about dumping Mike, an insanely loud engine roared up behind them, making them all uneasy.

"What is that?" yelled the driver.

As the motorcycle drew up next to the car, they saw it was Mike. His eyes were red, and he had a sinister smile on his face.

The jock said, in an astonished voice, "Is that Mike? What's going on? Where did he get that bike?"

Suddenly the motorcycle moved towards the car, and Mike smashed the driver's window with his bare hand. Blood gushed from his hand, and he laughed like a madman. The other guys were screaming in horror as the car swerved. Mike went at it again, and this time, he grabbed the driver by the hair. He pulled him with abnormal strength, and the guy's eye was cut open by the broken glass. The car lost all control and flew off the road, smashing into large rocks. Everyone inside died instantly. The motorcycle continued towards the mountain road.

About this time, Paul and his dog Soma were on their way back from a camping trip. Paul was listening to his favorite country music and drinking soda to stay awake. Soma heard the sound of the demonic engine and began to whimper.

"It's okay, boy. We will be home soon." Paul petted the dog on the head. But then he, too, heard the roaring engine and could see the headlight of the motorcycle zooming toward them at a very high speed.

As the crazy motorcycle drew up next to them and attempted to intimidate them, Paul quickly moved to his right before a sharp turn. The motorcycle was struck violently and flew off the mountain road. Mike, however, was thrown clear and landed in some bushes.

Paul did not take any chances and didn't stop to check anything. The motorcycle exploded in the ravine below the road. Mike slowly crawled out of the brush. Almost as if awakened from a dream, he stood on the mountain road, looking around with confusion.

Even when he heard what had happened to his fair-weather friends the next day, he had no idea the part he'd played in their demise. All he remembered was the guys dumping him on the side of the road.

His parents told him a guardian angel had protected him that night, while alcohol was to blame for the other guys' fatal crash.

Charles of the towing company never did find that motorcycle, but he didn't make much of an effort to look around. Shrugging, he calmly returned home that night and went to bed.

CHAPTER 18
NOT A FAN OF ART

The Order of the Crimson Owl's existence stretched all the way back to medieval times. Before that, it was known by different names and was spread among many tiny groups.

However, hunting vampires was a dangerous and extraordinary business. It became too difficult for small groups to operate well, so as Christians of old once held big councils, so did all of the vampire hunter organizations. They decided to combine into one, as the Order of the Crimson Owl and agreed to be partners with the Vatican. Having such a rich and powerful ally allowed the hunters to train full-time and to learn how to investigate efficiently and quickly. It became common for the hunters to learn ministry as well, but the use of things like holy water or the cross was simply a myth. These things did nothing to vampires.

In fact, many vampires were Christians themselves. Absurd as it sounds, being a vampire was simply a very rare disease that transformed and changed a human being. Those afflicted with it were actually still human, and just as there were those who abused power or were serial killers among humans, there were vampires who did the same things.

One story from fiction was true indeed. Sunlight could burn a vampire's skin in a terrible way; however, a vampire could probably survive in sunlight for a few hours before becoming completely drained and disfigured. Vampires could be killed with normal weapons, like all other humans; they were just much stronger and could handle injuries and wounds better.

Jus, one of the world's best vampire hunters, knew all of this very well. He knew that it didn't matter when he hunted the vampires. Because they were stronger at night, they never expected that hunters would go for them at night. So, Jus always had the edge.

The hunter had been watching the online presence of a certain masked Pierre for three months. Then the organization sent observers, people who checked out the person in question. They didn't send the hunters themselves to investigate each case, as there weren't that many of them. Most of the time, the observers came back, stating that the suspicions were unfounded.

Not this time. Jus sat by the window of his Paris apartment with the Eiffel Tower in the background. He was looking down at the summary of the report.

Pierre only holds events or meets people after 9 at night.

He is never seen during the daytime.

On several occasions, there seemed to be a shadow-like entity flying out of his window at night.

A young woman went missing after entering the house at night.

Dozens of dead animals drained of blood were found well-hidden after a long investigation.

No one had seen his face, though perhaps the missing young woman did.

Jus put down the paper. He usually avoided going after vampires who only killed animals. It meant they deliberately avoided killing humans. He simply felt that eliminating them was the wrong thing to do. He let other hunters take care of those. However, Pierre was a world-famous painter, something that had never happened with a vampire. They usually kept a low profile. This had really enraged the organization, and Jus was their number one hunter. He almost had no choice. Plus, there was a woman missing. The vampire had probably killed her; however, there was a chance she wanted to be a partner, and he'd turned her.

Either way, Jus had to do it. So, he was off to the place he hated the most. The airport.

Everything about the airport annoyed him. He hated crowds. Being alone and quiet was his preference; that's how he hunted, as well. They called him the silent hunter. Even vampires, with all of their heightened senses, sometimes missed him.

After getting through the airport, Jus headed to his second most-hated place. The airplane. He hated heights. Which made him sometimes wonder why he kept going with this profession. It was true that he had been raised to be a vampire hunter and knew nothing else, but he often searched for a sign indicating it was time to retire from this way of life and do something else.

Jus kept his eyes covered the entire flight. Upon his arrival, a car was waiting for him.

The farther he got from the big city, the better he felt. Gravil was a town located close to the mountains, but what was more incredible was that it also had vast forests, fields, lakes, rivers, and waterfalls. The driver told him that Gravil was getting some national news as a serial killer was operating there. This saddened Jus, but he instantly knew that it wasn't the vampire. This simply made him long more for retirement. Humans like that one were bigger monsters than most of the vampires he put down. Including the one, he was about to end.

Jus was given a room in a small hotel at the edge of the forest, which was, of course, strategic. The organization knew what he liked to do.

Luckily for Jus, Pierre had relaxed a lot these days and wasn't suspecting anyone. So when he heard the faint cries for help of someone lost near the lake one late night, his curiosity got the best of him, and he flew over to check what was going on.

The moon was full, beautiful and

bright. It was perfectly reflected upon the icy lake. Pierre landed near a tree and looked around. The sounds were gone. He heard a quick sound behind him, but before he could react, pain shot through his body as he was thrown against the tree. Some kind of chain with sharp long nails was at his waist, partially impaling him to the tree. As he grabbed at it, a strong voice stopped him.

"Don't even think about it, or I'll blow your head off right now."

A man in a long coat stood about ten meters away. He had a large gun pointed at Pierre. The vampire quit struggling. "You have finally found me," he said, resignedly.

Jus had to know. "Why did you paint? Why become so famous?"

"Why not use my talent, my creativity...I am not a monster. I live, I love, I feel...."

The man came closer. "Did you kill that woman who went missing after your gallery show?"

Pierre was silent for a moment, then his eyes filled with tears. Jus had never witnessed this before, and his hand slightly trembled.

"Yes…." Pierre told the truth, and his voice shook. He knew, either way, the hunter would kill him. Why carry a lie with him to the grave?

Jus took a long and deep sigh. He took aim. Because Jus had become emotional as well, he did not notice Kevin, the guy who never slept, behind him. Kevin struck Jus on the head with a large branch, and as Jus fell, clutching his head, Kevin kicked his gun away. Pierre took this time to free himself and then vanished into the night. Jus got to his feet and took out a smaller gun, pointing it at Kevin. He was a human, and Jus could only kill those who directly served vampires who killed humans. However, he doubted this man was that.

"Why did you do that?"

Kevin was astonished. "Why? Why did I help a man who has donated millions to poor children in this area, a man who sponsored the rebuilding of burned-down farms, a man who was in charge of all the historical restorations here in Gravil and paid to clear our forests? Why that man?"

Jus slowly lowered the gun and then sat in the snow.

He had been looking for a sign to retire from this profession, and this was it.

CHAPTER 19
JUST A PEACEFUL LIFE

Dan was hurrying down the main street, ignoring anyone who greeted him, any smells, views, or scenery. He wasn't being rude. He was focused. Dan knew that if he didn't follow through with this now, he might not have the courage later, or he might even forget.

At the same time, Pirel was sitting in his office. He was swamped with paperwork. Outside, it was snowing, and to make matters worse, the forecast for daytime was a winter storm.

Pirel was under tremendous pressure. He was about to be removed from the case. The town had trusted him for many years, yet even the citizens had now lost any faith they had in his abilities.

He switched from one paper to another. He was barely sleeping. The night before, he had spent looking at the online profiles of various people living in the town, but what if it was someone from another nearby town?

The headache was crushing him, and he was about to give up.

His assistant knocked and cracked open the door. "Mr. Pirel, a man named Dan is here to see you."

"I got no time."

"He says he knows who the killer is."

Pirel remained motionless for a moment, then his eyebrow twitched.

"Let…him in."

Moments later, Dan timidly stepped into the room and closed the door behind him. Pirel pointed to the seat across the desk. "Please, sit. What's your name?"

"Dan." Dan sat down and looked very nervous.

"Dan, why do you think you know who the killer is?" Pirel said, leaning back in his chair.

"I used to be a detective. It's a hunch based on observation. I saw a man follow the girl who ended up dead. The latest victim."

Pirel sat up straight. "That's better than what I've got. Who was it?"

"Thing is, I don't know his name."

Pirel let out a sigh of disappointment and sank back down, covering his head.

"But he wears all white and is tall, very handsome, in his thirties."

Pirel sat still for a while and then raised his head. "Wait…could it be…he's always greeting me in town…."

Pirel quickly typed on his computer and then turned the screen to Dan. Dan's face lit up.

"That's him!"

Pirel looked at the report.

"Usseti   Brianccinno…everything on him…is classified."

Pirel stood up for a moment and paced back and forth. Then he smacked his hands upon the table in front of Dan. The witness moved back a bit, frightened.

"Dan! Dan!" Pirel grabbed Dan by the shoulders and shook him. Dan was really terrified. "Dan the man!"

Pirel sat back down and grabbed his phone. Dan heard him calling all officers available.

"Dan. This guy must have been a top-secret assassin. I had a friend who worked in special operations. He told me they use a heart attack gun. Dan, do you understand? That's how he killed victims quietly and from a distance. Then he checks to make sure no one's around and takes the left ear. That is the only explanation. I have to go, Dan, but you should consider coming back to the force." Pirel slapped Dan's shoulder in approval and left in a hurry.

Meanwhile, as the snow fell outdoors, an unsuspecting Usseti was at home. His precious album lay on the table next to him as he finished his meal. Usseti had grown bold. He felt untouchable, and because of this, he had broken his own rules and brought a victim's body home.

A young man lay dead next to the table. Usseti was going to bury him in his own backyard after taking the left ear. He placed the final bite of food into his mouth, washed his hands and face and got a sharp kitchen knife. A special ear for today. With a smile on his face, he lifted the victim's head.

Suddenly, he sensed something was not right. Was the sound just his imagination? He quickly ran to the front window. At least a dozen cars were drawing near his house, unable to get closer because of the snow. Police officers were getting out of the cars. Usetti saw Pirel running towards the house. Usseti ran out the side door.

Pirel found the start of the winter storm very inconvenient as they all tried to park. They stopped the cars as best they could, and he led the charge toward the house. As he ran towards it, crunching the snow beneath his feet, he saw Usseti running out from the side of the building towards the forest. Pirel didn't want to take any chances, even if he himself were to be charged. He shot several times. It seemed like one of the bullets found its mark as Usseti stumbled, yet then got back up and kept running. The storm intensified, and it was hard to see. In a few minutes, vision was limited to just a few meters.

"Let him run towards the mountains. It's too cold. He won't get away. We will get him later," yelled one of the cops.

"No chance! Are you crazy? You all follow me! There!"

Pirel pointed at the blood on the snow; however, they had to move fast, as the blood was being covered up in a hurry. Like a mad hunting dog, Pirel was moving through the storm as fast as he could. He wasn't going to lose this man, no matter what.

The pursuit now led to the foot of the mountain. Everyone was following

Pirel as he circled around some large rocks. More blood. Pirel continued relentlessly.

Then the blood trail vanished. The others saw that Pirel was lost. However, he wasn't stopping. It was freezing, and yet they still continued searching for Usseti. An hour passed. The others were yelling something to Pirel, but he didn't care—he was going to get his man.

Several more hours passed. The storm had stopped, and Pirel's men were exhausted, pleading with him to go back. Yet, he would have none of it.

And then, after rounding a tall rocky formation, Pirel stopped. He took a deep breath and sighed, bending over. Usseti sat dead against a large rock. In his hand was one final ear. His own left ear.

Several months passed. Winter was over, and new life was springing up all around. Gravil was alive...and finally truly peaceful. Pirel walked upon the cobblestoned main street. He wasn't sure yet how he felt. So many lives had been lost during that dark period. Some viewed him as a villain who should have figured it out much earlier, and others hailed him as a hero.

However, he viewed himself as a simple man who tried his best and had ups and downs, just like anyone else out there. There were times when he thought he could have prevented more deaths, but then there were also times when he was happy and grateful that Dan had suddenly shown up at his office that day. It could have been much, much worse.

Pirel passed by the Mirrel family's jello café and smiled. He also greeted the hunter Paul, who was walking his dog, Soma.

Finally, he reached that old house. He cautiously entered and waited. There was no sense of death, no presence. The ghost had departed to another world. Pirel went into the dining room and sat by the window. Far away, he could see mountain peaks.

Very late that night, in the midst of those mountain peaks, a light went on inside a tiny house.

Two friends sat around a wooden table. Kevin, the man who never slept, and Pierre, the vampire. Kevin was drinking wine…and Pierre, well….

On the wall hung a gorgeous new painting of mountains.

Gravil was peaceful once again, indeed.

THE END

Alexander Semenyuk, (also known as Oleksandr Semenyuk) is a Ukrainian-American author. He was born in Lutsk, Ukraine, in 1986. At 14, he immigrated to the United States. Alexander's favorite genres are sci-fi, horror and fantasy. Early in life, Alexander was greatly influenced by classic literature and, since childhood, dreamed of becoming a writer.